TRAINS EAST	TRAINS WEST
5:32	6:16
6:02	7:59
7:11	8:47
8:49	:34
9:31	:58

A NOTE TO PARENTS

When your children are ready to "step into reading," giving them the right books—and lots of them—is as crucial as giving them the right food to eat. **Step into Reading Books** present exciting stories and information reinforced with lively, colorful illustrations that make learning to read fun, satisfying, and worthwhile. They are priced so that acquiring an entire library of them is affordable. And they are beginning readers with an important difference—they're written on four levels.

Step 1 Books, with their very large type and extremely simple vocabulary, have been created for the very youngest readers. **Step 2 Books** are both longer and slightly more difficult. **Step 3 Books,** written to mid-second-grade reading levels, are for the child who has acquired even greater reading skills. **Step 4 Books** offer exciting nonfiction for the increasingly proficient reader.

Children develop at different ages. **Step into Reading Books,** with their four levels of reading, are designed to help children become good—and interested—readers *faster*. The grade levels assigned to the four steps—preschool through grade 1 for Step 1, grades 1 through 3 for Step 2, grades 2 and 3 for Step 3, and grades 2 through 4 for Step 4—are intended only as guides. Some children move through all four steps very rapidly; others climb the steps over a period of several years. These books will help your child "step into reading" in style!

For Railroad Bill Griffith—
long may he chug!

Library of Congress Cataloging-in-Publication Data:

Schade, Susan. Railroad toad / by Susan Schade and Jon Buller. p. cm. – (Step into reading. A Step 1 book) SUMMARY: A fun-loving toad likes nothing better than to ride the train to unknown destinations. ISBN 0-679-83934-8 (pbk.) – ISBN 0-679-93934-2 (lib. bdg.) [1. Toads–Fiction. 2. Railroads–Trains–Fiction.] I. Buller, Jon. II. Title. III. Series: Step into reading. Step 1 book. PZ8.3.S287Rai 1993 [E]–dc20 92-23303

Manufactured in the United States of America   12   13   14   15   16   17   18   19   20

STEP INTO READING is a trademark of Random House, Inc.

Step into Reading

RAILROAD TOAD

A Step 1 Book

By Susan Schade
and Jon Buller

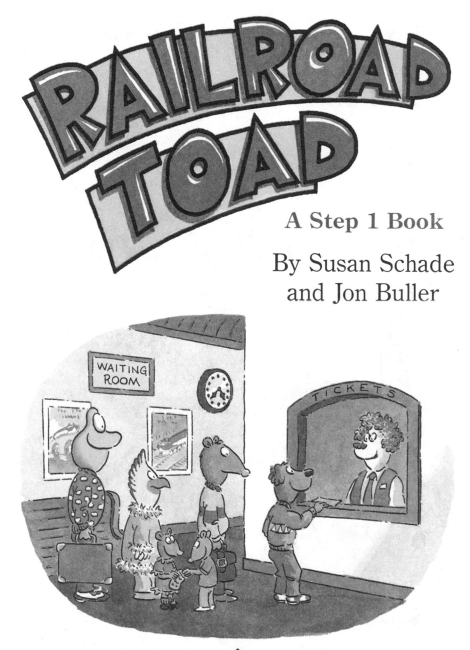

Random House 🏠 New York

I park my car
by the side of the road.
I grab my bag.
I'm…

RAILROAD TOAD!

Give me a ticket
to anywhere.
The farther the better.
I don't care!

Clang clang clang!
The train is coming.

Brakes are screeching.

Rails are humming.

I put my suitcase
on the rack.
The train starts moving
down the track.

Faster, faster,
we lurch and sway.
Whoosh! goes a train
the other way!

"Tickets, please."
Punch punch punch.

Chips and candy.
Munch munch munch.

We cross the river.
What a view!

We come to a tunnel.

We roar right through!

I make new friends.
Hello! Hello!

We see the train
from top to toe.
Diner...

dome car...

lounge car...

sleeper.

I take coach
because it's cheaper.

I nod off here.

I wake up there.

I stop to visit
Bug and Bear.

We play some golf.

We eat some pie.

We laugh a lot.

We say good-bye.

Next stop Maine.

Then...Mexico!

I'm Railroad Toad.
I love to GO!